How Do You Do?

Larissa Theule

illustrated by
Gianna Marino

BLOOMSBURY
CHILDREN'S BOOKS

NEW YORK LONDON OXFORD NEW DELHI SYDNEY

The day was hot.
The day before had also been hot.
And the day before that.
And the day before *that*.

When one is all the time hot,
days grow long and the world small,
because all one can think is . . .
It's hot.

Water Buffalo licked a drop of sweat
off his lip.
Crane aired out her wings.

Water Buffalo brushed away a fly with his tail.
Crane tried to eat the fly, but it was too fast
and flew away.

"Ah," said Water Buffalo.

"Ah," said Crane.

"Oh," said Water Buffalo.
"Oh," said Crane.
Every day the same.
Until . . .

"How do you do?" said someone new.
The two friends looked at each other.

They looked behind.
"How do you do?" said a goat.
"Hot," said Water Buffalo.

Goat licked him on the nose.
She licked Crane on the head.
That was unexpected!

"How do you do?" Goat said again. "How do *you* do, friend?" Crane asked kindly.

Then, as sudden as summer rain,
Goat started dancing.
Crane gasped. "That is so lovely!"

Water Buffalo snorted.

Crane tried a *shimmy*.

Water Buffalo sighed. But his knees bent.
Then his head bobbed.
He flipped his tail in time.

Goat crossed the field.
Crane followed Goat.
Water Buffalo followed Crane.

They forgot the sun.

They forgot the heat.

Had the earth ever smelled so sweet?

They danced on through the bushes,

on through the trees,

on to the next field over.

Water Buffalo led.

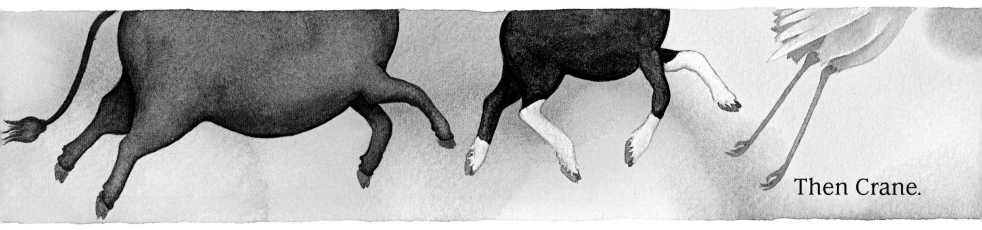

Then Crane.

Then Goat again.

The sun winked between the leaves.

And, as sudden as the summer rain,
Goat stopped dancing.

She kicked up her heels and took off,
growing small in the distance.

The earth stood still,

quiet,

luminous.

"Crane, that butterfly!"
"Ah!"

"Water Buffalo, see these flowers?"
"Oh!"

Crane felt a tingle from the dancing in her knees and a different kind of tingle in her heart.

"Do you know, meeting someone new makes the world feel not so—"

"Hot," said Water Buffalo.

"Yes," agreed Crane. "Nor so small."

"How do you do?"

"How do you do?"

They danced home,

inventing steps

of their own.

Who knew what

tomorrow might bring?

It would be hot . . .

But there were
dances to dance,
fields to visit,
and new friends to meet.

For my dearest Eero —L. T.

For all the people around the world
who have shown me a more gentle side of life
—G. M.

BLOOMSBURY CHILDREN'S BOOKS
Bloomsbury Publishing Inc., part of Bloomsbury Publishing Plc
1385 Broadway, New York, NY 10018

BLOOMSBURY, BLOOMSBURY CHILDREN'S BOOKS, and the Diana logo are trademarks of Bloomsbury Publishing Plc

First published in the United States of America in January 2019 by Bloomsbury Children's Books

Text copyright © 2019 by Larissa Theule
Illustrations copyright © 2019 by Gianna Marino

Bloomsbury books may be purchased for business or promotional use. For information on bulk purchases please
contact Macmillan Corporate and Premium Sales Department at specialmarkets@macmillan.com

Library of Congress Cataloging-in-Publication Data
Names: Theule, Larissa, author. | Marino, Gianna, illustrator.
Title: How do you do? / by Larissa Theule ; illustrated by Gianna Marino.
Description: New York : Bloomsbury, 2019.
Summary: All Water Buffalo and Crane can think about is how hot it is, day after day, until Goat arrives,
dancing and leading them on an adventure.
Identifiers: LCCN 2018010843 (print) | LCCN 2018017643 (e-book)
ISBN 978-1-61963-807-5 (hardcover) • ISBN 978-1-61963-808-2 (e-book) • ISBN 978-1-61963-809-9 (e-PDF)
Subjects: | CYAC: Habit—Fiction. | Heat—Fiction. | Water buffalo—Fiction. | Cranes (Birds)—Fiction. | Goats—Fiction.
Classification: LCC PZ7.T3526 How 2019 (print) | LCC PZ7.T3526 (e-book) | DDC [E]—dc23
LC record available at https://lccn.loc.gov/2018010843

Illustrations created with gouache on watercolor paper
Typeset in Usherwood Medium
Book design by Heather Palisi
Printed in China by Leo Paper Products, Heshan, Guangdong
2 4 6 8 10 9 7 5 3 1

All papers used by Bloomsbury Publishing Plc are natural, recyclable products made from wood grown in well-managed forests.
The manufacturing processes conform to the environmental regulations of the country of origin.

To find out more about our authors and books visit www.bloomsbury.com and sign up for our newsletters.

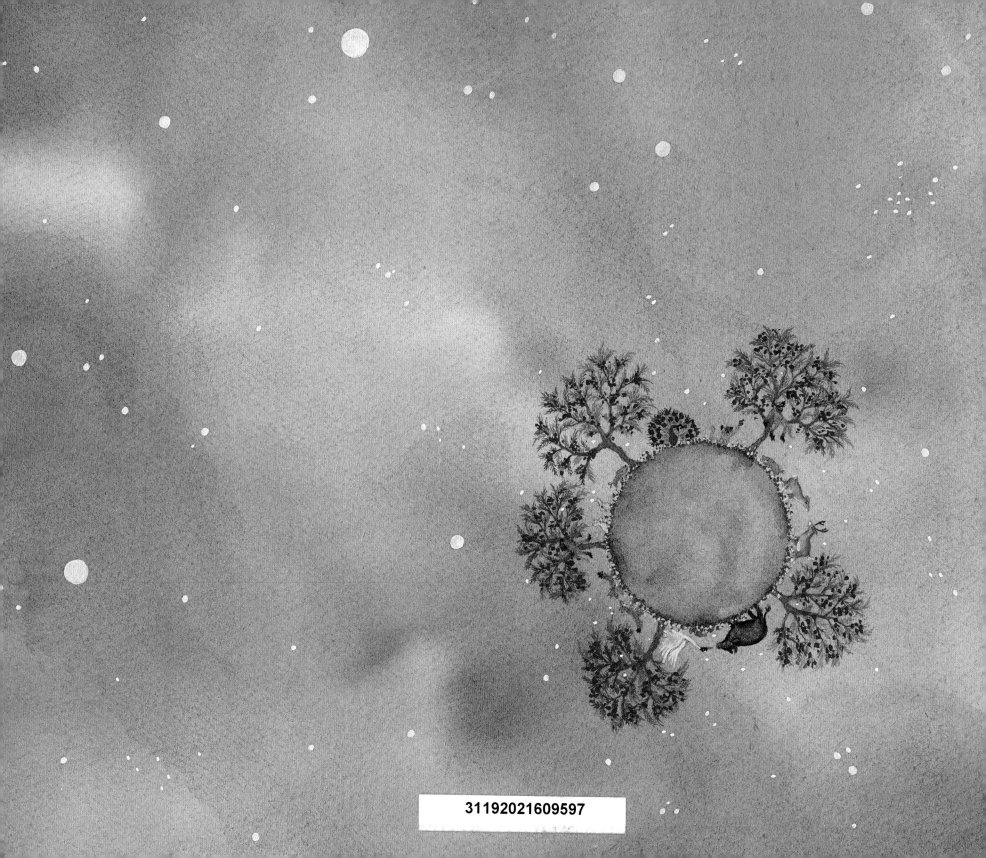